MW00762901

This Book Belongs To:

_____

That's What Matters Most

Copyright ©2022 Little Hippo Books

All rights reserved. No part of this publication may be reproduced, distributed, or transmitted in any form or by any means, including photocopying, recording, or other electronic or mechanical methods, without the prior permission of the publisher, except in the case of brief quotations embodied in critical reviews and certain other non-commercial uses permitted by copyright law.

For permissions contact:
info@littlehippobooks.com

ISBN: 978-1-958774-44-1

Illustrations by Hazel Quintanilla.
Story written by Jennifer Waddle.
In Consultation with Dr. Nikki Fynn.

First printing edition 2022.

Little Hippo
Books

www.littlehippobooks.com

THAT'S WHAT MATTERS MOST

What do you think about yourself - how you look, how you act, and how you feel?

Have you ever heard of **self-esteem?** It's something very real! It means being confident and having good thoughts, about who you are and the talents you've got.

You see, there's no one in the world like you, so you can feel proud of the things you do.

Even when you make a mistake, just admit it - and know it's okay!

Always remind yourself of what is true, and keep on being a wonderful you!

When reading this book, have some paper and a pen next to you so you can jot down what makes you smart, what you like about yourself, and how you feel about the different topics discussed.

Tips for Reading:

Follow these tips to help keep your child engaged while reading.

- Have fun while you read! Use different voices for the different characters.

- Ask questions about the pages you just read.

- Point out fun objects in the art.

- Make reading part of your bedtime ritual.

- Use this as a resource or a reminder of helpful tips for when you are feeling embarrassed or have low-self esteem.

Feelings And Emotions:

"How are you feeling?" is a question asked almost every single day. When you can learn to identify your feelings specifically, you will be able to learn how to respond more accurately. Not only is it helpful for others to understand what is going on inside of you, it is helpful for you to know what is going on inside of yourself. The more specific you can be in labeling your feelings and emotions, the more understanding you will have for yourself.

A Feelings Wheel is a tool developed by Robert Plutchik and is used to help recognize and communicate feelings. At the center of the wheel are "core" emotions. These are emotions that are more easily identified or expressed, such as joy, sadness, and anger. More complex emotions, such as isolated, pleased and aggravated, are on the outer edge. After choosing the most accurate core emotion, run your finger along the pie slice to try to pinpoint a more specific emotion. These more specific emotions are what you can explain to others so that they have a deeper understanding of what you are experiencing. This can help you to open up instead of hiding behind what is the easy or standard answer.

So, how are you feeling today?

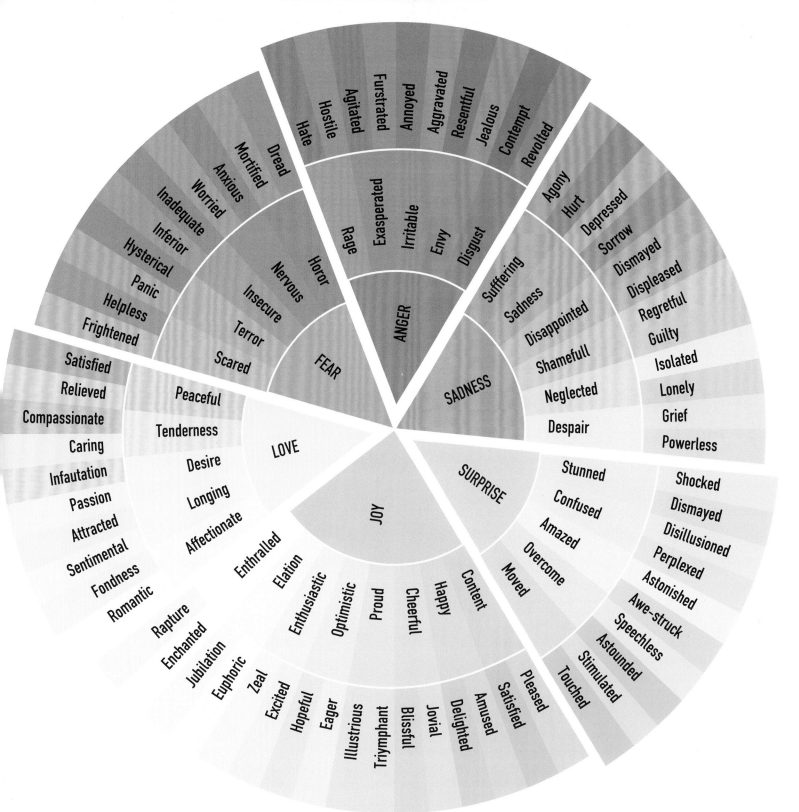

When I do things right, everyone says,
"Great job! Keep it up!"

I like how this makes me feel, so I try to do
everything right - like getting straight As in school.

I know straight As aren't the only way to show
I'm smart and I need to remember that. Otherwise,
if I don't get an A, it will be easy to feel like a failure.

The next time this happens, and I don't get an A, I'll ask myself,
"Are you smart?"

Of course, the answer is yes! I am smart and
I work hard in school. And THAT'S what matters most!

When I show talent, and the audience cheers, it makes me feel amazing!
Like the time I did a backflip from the high dive at the swimming meet.

However, sometimes I don't swim very fast and I take last place. This makes me feel like I've let my team down. I know if I want to swim faster, I might just have to practice. Some people on our team are faster than me. Maybe they can give me some tips.

The next time this happens, and I don't come in first, I'll ask myself, "Are you a good swimmer?"

Of course, I am! I love swimming and go to practice every week. And THAT'S what matters most.

Sometimes, my brother and sister make me feel like I can't do anything right.

Like the time we went hiking and I couldn't climb up the steep hill. This made me feel small and weak.

Maybe I just need to exercise more and build my leg muscles so these hills become easier to climb.

The next time this happens, and I feel weak, I'll ask myself, "Am I a strong person?"

Of course, I am! Just because I had a hard time climbing one hill doesn't mean I am not strong. I am strong in many ways and one day I'll be able to climb that hill. And THAT'S what matters most!

My best friend doesn't always like what I wear, and sometimes, she criticizes me.

Like the time I wore my purple raincoat with my orange rain boots. She said, "Those colors don't match!"

At first, I felt embarrassed, but then I asked myself,
"Do you like these colors?"

Of course, the answer was yes! I love all the colors of the rainbow.
And THAT'S what matters most!

Sometimes, my friends do things I don't want to do, but I feel like I have to go along with them.

Like the time they built a clubhouse, but didn't let the new neighbor kid play.

I felt torn between my friends and my new neighbor.
Then, I asked myself, "Are you a kind person?"

Of course, the answer was yes! I am a kind person,
but that doesn't mean I have to do what others want
to do all the time. So, I chose to play with my new neighbor.
And THAT'S what matters most!

Sometimes, the bully at school says mean things and picks on me.

Like the time he chased me up the slide and stood at the bottom so I couldn't slide down! It made me feel unlikable.

Then, I remembered that bullies have low self-esteem, which means they don't like themselves so they pick on others.

I asked myself, "Are you a likable person?"

Of course, I am! Besides, how one person feels about me is not as important as how I feel about me. And THAT'S what matters most!

When I ignore what makes me happy, and always try to make others happy, I start to feel down.

Like when I pretend to like arts and crafts when I would rather play outside.

Maybe the next time we can do something they want to do for a while and then do something I want to do.
(This would be the honest thing to do.)

The next time this happens, I'll ask myself,
"How can I be honest about what makes me happy?"

Of course, it's important to do things that make you happy, too!
And THAT'S what matters most!

What you think about yourself is important.

It builds your **self-esteem**.

And all it takes is reminding yourself that you are **smart, strong, kind,** and **likable**.

There's no one quite like you!

AND THAT'S WHAT MATTERS MOST

Tips To Help Achieve Good Self-Esteem

- A simple act, such as coloring or drawing, takes your attention away from yourself (and those things that are stressing you out!) and onto the present-moment event.

- Practice confidence. Don't worry about what others think or say about you.

- Do not get discouraged if you cannot do something on the first try. Use that 3-letter word "YET." Instead of saying, "I can't ride a bike," say "I can't ride a bike, yet." This turns a NO WAY into a MAYBE.

- When your friends want to do something different from you, ask yourself, "Will doing what they want make me happy?" It is important to know what makes YOU happy because it may be different from what makes others happy.

- Make a "Wins" list and write down all the things you are good at and have accomplished. If there is something missing from your list that you like to do, but aren't so good at, such as swimming or hiking, put those on a "Wish" list. Once you've accomplished the things on your Wish list, move them over to your Wins list.

Discussion Questions
About Self-Esteem for Children

1. What was the last thing you did that you were proud of?

2. How does it make you feel when someone praises you? Does it feel different if it comes from a family member or a friend?

3. What do you like about yourself?

4. Are there things that you do not like about yourself? How can you change that?

5. Do you think you have high or low self-esteem?

6. What makes you smart?

Self-Esteem Word Search

```
L R G Q V R E D N A J S X T T
O G P E Q V M B J S J C K R Z
F E E L I N G S E K T E C U E
G I Z U S O B C B L N R H T T
P D F H J E P O C C I W O H W
P I M J R R L N P K U E D N M
D G W O R T H F Q E N Q V Y G
F N K U F F R I E V Q R W E B
L I R W H N E D T S Q E W A X
Q T E V S L B E D B T C T V Y
R Y S J V U X N B U B E C C W
P S P Q J H S C L P I E E R N
L E E G L S Z E E B A F C M B
V S C F A E G H L W E U K L R
S S T P Q P A T I E N C E W J
```

Word Bank:

Self Esteem	Strong	Confidence	Worth	Dignity
Patience	Truth	Believe	Feelings	Respect

Dr. Nikki Fynn, Consultant

With over 20 years of experience working in schools and communities, Nikki obtained her doctorate degree in educational leadership at Appalachian State University. She is a consultant for relational education services that entail art-based learning, inclusion, trauma-informed education, and social-emotional learning. Nikki is a professor at Appalachian State University where she teaches Inclusion to student teachers in the special education department. She also works 1-1 with students as a social-emotional academic learning coach, and provides trainings/workshops for professionals who work with children of divorce and family trauma.

In addition to content writing for organizations, Nikki has also published digital lesson plans and other products that she sells on Amazon, Gumroad, and Barnes and Noble. She has also been published in Edutopia. Nikki is a single mom who believes that learning must be student-centered to foster engagement and meaningful learning among students.

More From Little Hippo Books

I Am Okay

We all have feelings and feelings aren't bad. We all feel scared, angry, nervous and sad. What matters is how we handle our feelings. Read along and learn a few tips and tricks on identifying and coping with feelings.

The Big Cookie Mess Up

Everyone makes mistakes. No one is perfect. What you do after you make a mistake is what is important. Read along and learn some tips from Emma as she works through the big cookie mess up that she created.

What Does Brave Look Like?

We have all heard the expression, "That was brave," but do you really know what brave means? Being brave means doing something even though you may feel scared. In this story, Julian's bravery is tested by taking off the training wheels on his bicycle.

Everyone Gets Embarrassed

Feeling embarrassed isn't much fun, but the truth is, it happens to all of us! Help your child learn to handle embarrassing situations with confidence. After all, everyone gets embarrassed!

Little Hippo
Books

Sign up to see what's new at littlehippobooks.com.

Follow us on social media to stay up to date on the latest from Little Hippo Books.

 @LittleHippoBooks

 @LittleHippoBooks

 Little Hippo Books